SISKIYOU COUNTY LIBRARY
3 2871 00214473 7

D0792301

LUNCH WITH MILLY

LUNCH WITH MILLY

by Jeanne Modesitt
pictures by Robin Spowart

BridgeWater Books

Published by BridgeWater Books,
an imprint of Troll Associates, Inc.

Printed in Mexico.
10 9 8 7 6 5 4 3 2 1

Library of Congress Cataloging-in-Publication Data
Modesitt, Jeanne.
Lunch with Milly / by Jeanne Modesitt;
pictures by Robin Spowart.
p. cm.
Summary: Milly and her friend meet a fox, a turtle, and a
frog, who give them the ingredients for a splendid dessert.
ISBN 0-8167-3388-0
[1. Desserts—Fiction. 2. Animals—Fiction.]
I. Spowart, Robin, ill. II. Title.
PZ7.M715Lu 1995 [E]—dc20 93-33808

To Emily
and Mikoh
with all
our love.

One day I invited my friend Milly over for lunch.

I made sandwiches that had peanut butter, banana, and sunflower seeds on the inside.

"Delicious!" said Milly after she had finished her sandwich. "What's for dessert?"

"Oh, no!" I said. "I forgot to make dessert."

"No matter," said Milly. "I know where we can get some dessert." She picked up a small pail in one hand and took my hand in the other.

"Ready?" she asked.

"Ready," I said.

And out the window we flew.

In a short while, we landed on a sandy shore.

"Now then," said Milly. "Now you must sing. You must sing a song of cats and ships. For the fox."

"Ohhh," I said. I didn't know any songs about cats and ships, so I made one up.

"My cats ran away
so they could go sailing,
sailing the deep, blue sea.
My cats ran away
so they could go sailing,
but now they've come back to me."

The moment I finished singing, I heard a deep sigh. And then another.

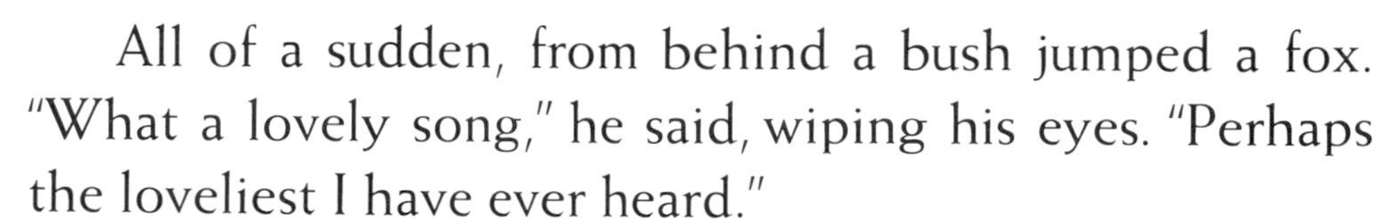

All of a sudden, from behind a bush jumped a fox. "What a lovely song," he said, wiping his eyes. "Perhaps the loveliest I have ever heard."

The fox opened his satchel and pulled out a large handful of strawberries. "Please," he said, "won't you help yourself to some strawberries?"

"Why, thank you, fox," I said, taking the berries and putting them into the pail.

"You're welcome," said the fox. He turned to go. "Good-bye. And thank you again for such a lovely song."

"Good-bye." Milly and I waved.

"Now then," said Milly. "Now you must dance. You must dance the dance of seaweed. For the turtle."

"Ohhh," I said. I didn't know how to dance the dance of seaweed. I had never done it before. I closed my eyes and imagined I was a piece of seaweed swaying in the salty water. Swaying, swaying…

"Bravo!" came a voice. I opened my eyes. A large sea turtle was standing on the shore, looking directly at me. "Never in my one hundred years," continued the turtle, "have I seen anyone dance the dance of seaweed as wonderfully as you."

Suddenly the turtle turned toward the water and dove under a wave. A moment later she reappeared on shore. On top of her back was a glass jar filled with lemons.

"Please," said the turtle, "won't you help yourself to a lemon?"

"Why, thank you, turtle," I said, opening the jar and taking a lemon.

"You're welcome," said the turtle. She moved toward the water. "Good-bye. And thank you again for a truly wonderful dance."

"Good-bye." Milly and I waved.

"Now then," said Milly. "Now you must act. You must act the part of a queen. For the frog."

"Ohhh," I said. I had never been a queen before. I bent down and picked several yellow flowers and put them in my hair. Then I lifted my head high, and with a grand stride walked around in the sand.

"Splendid performance!" came the voice of a frog, sitting on top of a rock. "Absolutely splendid!"

The frog hopped off the rock and into a hole. A moment later he reappeared with a plateful of fresh mint leaves. "Please," said the frog, "won't you help yourself to some mint?"

"Why, thank you, frog," I said, taking some leaves.

"You're welcome," said the frog, hopping away. "Good-bye. And thank you again for a most splendid performance."

"Good-bye." Milly and I waved.

I looked down at the strawberries, the lemon, and the mint leaves. "Milly," I said. "I think I can make us some dessert now."

"Good!" said Milly.

She took my hand and back home we flew...

to eat a lovely,
wonderful,
splendid
dessert.

Strawberries with Lemon and Mint

1 quart strawberries, washed and hulled
juice of 1/2 lemon
1 tablespoon sugar
5 fresh mint leaves, torn into tiny bits

Put the strawberries in a large bowl. Add the lemon juice, sugar, and mint leaves. Toss gently. Cover and let stand for about 20 minutes in the refrigerator to allow the flavors to mingle. Serve and enjoy!